Elves and Heroes

Donald A. MacKenzie

ELVES AND HEROES

BY

DONALD A. MACKENZIE.

1909

TO

Miss YULE, of TARRADALE.

PREFACE.

THE ELVES.

The immemorial folk-beliefs of our native land are passing away, but they still retain for us a poetic appeal, not only on account of the glamour of early associations, but also because they afford us inviting glimpses of the mental habits and inherent characteristics of the men and women of past generations. When we re-tell the old tales of our ancestors, we sit beside them over the peat-fire; and, as we glory with them in their strong heroes, and share their elemental joys and fears, we breathe the palpitating air of that old mysterious world of theirs, peopled by spirits beautiful, and strange, and awe-inspiring.

The attitude of the Gael towards the supernatural, and his general outlook upon life in times gone by, was not associated with unbroken gloom; nor was he always an ineffectual dreamer and melancholy fatalist. These attributes belong chiefly to the Literary Celt of latter-day conception—the Celt of Arnold and Renan, and other writers following in their wake, who have woven misty impressions of a people whom they have met as strangers, and never really understood. Celtic literature is not a morbid literature. In Highland poetry there is more light than shadow, much symbolism, but no vagueness; pictures are presented in minute detail; stanzas are cunningly wrought in a spirit of keen artistry; and the literary style is direct and clear and comprehensible. In Highland folklore we find associated with the haunting "fear of things invisible, " common to all peoples in early stages of development, a confident feeling of security inspired by the minute observances of ceremonial practices. We also note a distinct tendency to discriminate between spirits, some of which are invariably friendly, some merely picturesque, and perhaps fearsome, and others constantly harbouring a desire to work evil upon mankind. Associated with belief in the efficacy of propitiatory offerings and "ceremonies of riddance, " is the ethical suggestion that good wishes and good deeds influence spirits to perform acts of kindly intent.

Of fairies the Highlanders spoke, as they are still prone to do in these districts where belief in them is not yet extinct, with no small degree of regard and affection. It may be that "the good folk" and the "peace-people" (*sitchean*) were so called that good intention might be compelled by the conjuring influence of a name, as well as to avoid giving offence by uttering real names, as if it were desired to exercise a magical influence by their use. Be that as it may, it is evident from Highland folk-tales that the fairies were oftener the friends than the foes of mankind. When men and women were lured to their dwellings they rarely suffered injury; indeed, the fairies appeared to have taken pleasure in their company. To such as they favoured they imparted the secrets of their skill in the arts of piping, of swordmaking, etc. At sowing time or harvest they were at the service of human friends. On the needy they took pity. They never failed in a promise; they never forgot an act of kindness, which they invariably rewarded seven-fold. Against those who wronged them they took speedy vengeance. It would appear that on these humanised spirits of his conception the Highlander left, as one would expect him to do, the impress of his own character—his shrewdness and high sense of honour, his love of music and gaiety, his warmth of heart and love of comrades, and his indelible hatred of tyranny and wrong.

The Highland "wee folk" are not so diminutive as the fairies of England—at least that type of fairy, beloved of the poet, which hovers bee-like over flowers and feeds on honey-dew. Power they had to shrink in stature and to render themselves invisible, but they are invariably "little people, " from three to four feet high. It may be that the Gael's conception of humanised spirits may not have been uninfluenced by the traditions of that earlier diminutive race whose arrow-heads of flint were so long regarded as "elf-bolts. " The fairies dwelt only in grassy knolls, on the summits of high hills, and inside cliffs. Although capable of living for several centuries, they were not immortal. They required food, and borrowed meal and cooking utensils from human beings, and always returned what they received on loan. They could be heard within the knolls grinding corn and working at their anvils, and they were adepts at spinning and weaving and harvesting. When they went on long journeys they became invisible, and were carried through the air on eddies of western wind.

At the seasonal changes of the year, "the wee folk" were for several days on end inspired, like all other supernatural furies, with enmity against mankind. Their evil influences were negatived by spells and charms. We who still hang on our walls at Christmas the mystic holly, are unconsciously perpetuating an old-world custom connected with belief in the efficacy of the magical circle to protect us against evil spirits. And in our concern about luck, our proneness to believe in omens, the influence of colours and numbers, in dreams and in prophetic warnings, we retain as much of the spirit as the poetry of the religion of our remote ancestors.

THE HEROES.

The heroes, with the exception of Cuchullin, who appear in this volume, figure in the tales and poems of the Ossianic or Fian Cycle, which is common to Ireland and to Scotland. They have been neglected by our Scottish poets since Gavin Douglas and Barbour. In Ireland the Fians are a band of militia—the original Fenians. In Scotland the tales vary considerably, and belong to the hunting period before the introduction of agriculture. But in this country, as well as in Ireland, they are evidently influenced by historic happenings. There are tales of Norse conflicts, as well as tales of adventure among giants and spirits.

The cycle had evidently remote beginnings. When we find Diarmid and Grainnè, like Paris and Helen, the cause of conflict and disaster; and Diarmid, like Achilles, charmed of body, and vulnerable only on his heel-spot, we incline to the theory that from a mid-European centre migrating "waves" swept over prehistoric Greece, and left traces of their mythology and folk-lore in Homer, while other "waves, " sweeping northward, bequeathed to us as a literary inheritance the Celtic folk-tales, in which the deeds and magical attributes of remote tribal heroes and humanised deities are co-mingled and perpetuated.

On fragments of these folk-tales the poet Macpherson reared his Ossianic epic, in imitation of the Iliad and Paradise Lost.

The "Death of Cuchullin" is a rendering in verse of an Irish prose translation of a fragment of the Cuchullin Cycle, which moves in the Bronze Age period. Cuchullin, with "the light of heroes" on his forehead, is also reminiscent of Achilles. One of the few Cuchullin tales found in Scotland is that which relates his conflict with his son, and bears a striking similarity to the legend of Sohrab and Rustum. Macpherson also drew from this Cycle in composing his Ossian, and mingled it with the other, with which it has no connection.

The third great Celtic Cycle—the Arthurian—bears close resemblances, as Campbell, of "The West Highland Tales, " has shown, to the Fian Cycle, and had evidently a common origin. Its value as a source of literary inspiration has been fully appreciated, but the Fian and Cuchullin cycles still await, like virgin soil, to yield an abundant harvest for the poets of the future.

Notes on the folk-beliefs and tales will be found at the end of this volume.

Some of the short poems have appeared in the "Glasgow Herald" and "Inverness Courier"; the three tales appeared in the "Celtic Review."

CONTENTS.

Preface

The Wee Folk

The Remnant Bannock

The Banshee

Conn, Son of the Red

The Song of Goll

The Blue Men of the Minch

The Urisk

The Nimble Men

My Gunna

The Gruagach

The Little Old Man of the Barn

Yon Fairy Dog

The Water-Horse

The Changeling

My Fairy Lover

The Fians of Knockfarrel

Her Evil Eye

A Cursing

Leobag's Warning

Tober Mhuire

Sleepy Song

Song of the Sea

The Death of Cuchullin

Lost Songs

OTHER POEMS.

The Dream

Free Will

Strife

Sonnet

"Out of the Mouths of Babes"

Notes

Elves and Heroes

THE WEE FOLK.

In the knoll that is the greenest,
  And the grey cliff side,
And on the lonely ben-top
  The wee folk bide;
They'll flit among the heather,
  And trip upon the brae—
The wee folk, the green folk, the red folk and grey.

As o'er the moor at midnight
  The wee folk pass,
They whisper 'mong the rushes
  And o'er the green grass;
All through the marshy places
  They glint and pass away—
The light folk, the lone folk, the folk that will not stay.

O many a fairy milkmaid
  With the one eye blind,
Is 'mid the lonely mountains
  By the red deer hind;
Not one will wait to greet me,
  For they have naught to say—
The hill folk, the still folk, the folk that flit away.

When the golden moon is glinting
  In the deep, dim wood,
There's a fairy piper playing
  To the elfin brood;
They dance and shout and turn about,
  And laugh and swing and sway—
The droll folk, the knoll folk, the folk that dance alway.

O we that bless the wee folk
  Have naught to fear,
And ne'er an elfin arrow
  Will come us near;
For they'll give skill in music,
  And every wish obey—
The wise folk, the peace folk, the folk that work and play.

Elves and Heroes

They'll hasten here at harvest,
  They will shear and bind;
They'll come with elfin music
  On a western wind;
All night they'll sit among the sheaves,
  Or herd the kine that stray—
The quick folk, the fine folk, the folk that ask no pay.

Betimes they will be spinning
  The while we sleep,
They'll clamber down the chimney,
  Or through keyholes creep;
And when they come to borrow meal
  We'll ne'er them send away—
The good folk, the honest folk, the folk that work alway.

O never wrong the wee folk—
  The red folk and green,
Nor name them on the Fridays,
  Or at Hallowe'en;
The helpless and unwary then
  And bairns they lure away—
The fierce folk, the angry folk, the folk that steal and slay.

BONNACH FALLAIDH.

(THE REMNANT BANNOCK.)

O, the good-wife will be singing
  When her meal is all but done—
Now all my bannocks have I baked,
  I've baked them all but one;
And I'll dust the board to bake it,
  I'll bake it with a spell—
O, it's Finlay's little bannock
  For going to the well.

The bannock on the brander
  Smells sweet for your desire—
O my crisp ones I will count not
  On two sides of the fire;
And not a farl has fallen
  Some evil to foretell!—
O it's Finlay's little bannock
  For going to the well.

The bread would not be lasting,
  'Twould crumble in your hand;
When fairies would be coming here
  To turn the meal to sand—
But what will keep them dancing
  In their own green dell?
O it's Finlay's little bannock
  For going to the well.

Now, not a fairy finger
  Will do my baking harm—
The little bannock with the hole,
  O it will be the charm.
I knead it, I knead it, 'twixt my palms,
  And all the bairns I tell—
O it's Finlay's little bannock
  For going to the well.

Elves and Heroes

THE BANSHEE.

Knee-deep she waded in the pool—
  The Banshee robed in green—
She sang yon song the whole night long,
  And washed the linen clean;
The linen that would wrap the dead
  She beetled on a stone,
She stood with dripping hands, blood-red,
  Low singing all alone—

His linen robes are pure and white,
For Fergus More must die to-night!

'Twas Fergus More rode o'er the hill,
  Come back from foreign wars,
His horse's feet were clattering sweet
  Below the pitiless stars;
And in his heart he would repeat—
  "O never again I'll roam;
All weary is the going forth,
  But sweet the coming home!"

His linen robes are pure and white,
For Fergus More must die to-night!

He saw the blaze upon his hearth
  Come gleaming down the glen;
For he was fain for home again,
  And rode before his men—
"'Tis many a weary day," he'd sigh,
  "Since I would leave her side;
I'll never more leave Scotland's shore
  And yon, my dark-eyed bride."

His linen robes are pure and white,
For Fergus More must die to-night!

So dreaming of her tender love,
  Soft tears his eyes would blind—
When up there crept and swiftly leapt

Elves and Heroes

A man who stabbed behind—
"'Tis you," he cried, "who stole my bride,
  This night shall be your last!" ...
When Fergus fell, the warm, red tide
  Of life came ebbing fast ...

His linen robes are pure and white,
For Fergus More must die to-night!

Elves and Heroes

CONN, SON OF THE RED.

The Fians sojourned by the shore
Of comely Cromarty, and o'er
The wooded hill pursued the chase
With ardour. 'Twas a full moon's space
Ere Beltane[1] rites would be begun
With homage to the rising sun—
Ere to the spirits of the dead
Would sacrificial blood be shed
In yon green grove of Navity—[2]
When Conn came over the Eastern Sea,
His heart aflame with vengeful ire,
To seek for Goll, who slew his sire
When he was seven years old.

    Finn saw
In dreams, ere yet he came, with awe
The Red One's son, so fierce and bold,
In combat with his hero old—
The king-like Goll of valorous might—
A stormy billow in the fight
No foe could ere withstand.

    He knew
The strange ship bore brave Conn, and blew
Clear on his horn the Warning Call;
And round him thronged the Fians all
With wond'ring gaze.

    The sun drew nigh
The bale-fires of the western sky,
And faggot clouds with blood-red glare,
Caught flame, and in the radiant air
Lone Wyvis like a jewel shone—
The Fians, as they stared at Conn,
Were stooping on the high Look-Out.
They watched the ship that tacked about,
Now slant across the firth, and now
Laid bare below the cliff's broad brow,
And heaving on a billowy steep,

Elves and Heroes

Like to a monster of the deep
That wallowed, labouring in pain—
And Conn stared back with cold disdain.

Pondering, he sat alone behind
The broad sail swallowing the wind,
As over the hollowing waves that leapt
And snarled with foaming lips, and swept
Around the bows in querulous fray,
And tossed in curves of drenching spray,
The belching ship with ardour drove;
Then like a lordly elk that strove
Amid the hounds and, charging, rent
The pack asunder as it went,
It bore round and in beauty sprang—
The sea-wind through the cordage sang
With high and wintry merriment
That stirred the heart of Conn, intent
On vengeance, and for battle keen—
So hard, so steadfast, and serene.

Then Ossian, sweet of speech, spake low,
With musing eyes upon the foe,
"Is Conn more noble than The Red,
Whom Goll in battle vanquished?"
"The Red was fiercer," Conan cried—
"Nay, Conn is nobler," Finn replied,
"More comely, stalwart, mightier far—
What sayest thou, Goll, my man of war?"
Then Goll made answer on the steep,
Nor ceased to gaze on Conn full deep—
"His equal never came before
Across the seas to Alban shore,
Nor ever have I peered upon
A nobler, mightier man than Conn"

The ship flew seaward, tacking wide,
Contending with the wind and tide,
And when upon the broad stream's track
It baffled hung, or drifted back,
With grunt and shriek, like battling boars,
The shock and swing of bladed oars
Came sounding o'er the sea

Elves and Heroes

    The dusk
Grew round the twilight, like a husk
That holds a kernel choice, and keen,
Cold stars impaled the sky serene,
When Conn's ship through the slackening tide
Drew round the wistful bay and wide,
Behind the headlands high that snout
The seas like giant whales, and spout
The salt foam high and loud

    Then sighed
The gasping men who all day plied
Their oars in plunging seas, with hands
Grown stiff, and arms, like twisted bands
Drawn numbly, as they rose outspent,
And staggering from their benches went
The sail napped quarrelling, and drank
The wind in broken gasps, and sank
With sullen pride upon the boards,
And smote the mast and shook the cords

Darkly loomed that alien land,
And darkly lowered the Fian band,
For hovering on the shoreland grey
The ship they followed round the bay
Nor sought the sheltering woods until
The shadows folded o'er the hill
Full heavily, and night fell blind,
And laid its spell upon the wind

The swelling waters sank with sip
And hollow gurgle round the ship,
The long mast rocked against the dim,
Soft heaven above the headland's rim

But while the seamen crouched to sleep,
Conn sat alone in reverie deep,
And saw before him in a maze
The mute procession of his days,
In gloom and glamour wending fast—
His heart a-hungering for the past—
Again he leapt, a tender boy,
To greet his sire with eager joy,

Elves and Heroes

When he came over the wide North Sea,
Enriched with spoils of victory—
Then heavily loomed that fateful morn
When tidings of his fall were borne
From Alban shore ... Again he saw
The youth who went alone with awe
To swear the avenging oath before
The smoking altar red with gore.

Ah! strange to him it seemed to be
That hour was drawing nigh when he
Would vengeance take ... And still more strange,
O sorrow! it would bring no change
Though blood for blood be spilled, and life
For life be taken in fierce strife;
'Twill ne'er recall the life long sped,
Or break the silence of the dead.

But when he heard his mother's wail,
Once more uplifted on the gale,
Moaning The Red who ne'er returned—
His cheeks with sudden passion burned;
And darkly frowned that valiant man,
As through his quivering body ran
The lightnings of impelling ire
And impulses of fierce desire,
That surged, with a consuming hate
Against a world made desolate,
Unceasing and unreconciled,
And ever clamouring ... like wild,
Dark-deeded waves that stun the shore,
And through the anguished twilight roar
The hungry passions of the wide
And gluttonous deep unsatisfied.

II.

The shredding dawn in beauty spread
Its shafts of splendour, golden-red,
High over the eastern heaven, and broke
Through flaking clouds in silvern smoke
That burst aflame, and fold o'er fold,
Let loose their oozing floods of gold,

Elves and Heroes

Splashed over the foamless deep that lay
Tremulous and clear. In fiery play
The rippling beams that swept between
The sea-cleft Sutor crags serene,
Broke quivering where the waters bore
The soft reflection of the shore.

The pipes of morn were sounding shrill
Through budding woods on plain and hill,
And stirred the air with song to wake
The sweet-toned birds within the brake.

The Fians from their sheilings came,
With offerings to the god a-flame,
And round them thrice they sun-wise went;
Then naked-kneed in silence bent
Beside the pillar stones ...

      But now
Brave Conn upon the ship's high prow
Hath raised his burnished blade on high,
And calls on Woden and on Tigh
With boldness, to avenge the death
Of his great sire ... In one deep breath
He drains the hero's draught that burns
With valour of the gods; then turns
His long-sought foe to meet ... Great Conn
Sweeps, stooping in a boat, alone.
Shoreward, with rapid blades and bright,
That shower the foam-rain pearly white,
And rip the waters, bending lithe,
In hollowing swirls that hiss and writhe
Like adders, ere they dart away
Bright-spotted with the flakes of spray.

When, furrowing the sand, he drew
His boat the shallowing water through,
A giant he in stature rose
Straight as a mast before his foes,
With head thrown high, and shoulders wide
And level, and set back with pride;
His bared and supple arms were long
As shapely oars: firm as a thong

Elves and Heroes

His right hand grasped his gleaming blade,
Gold-hilted, and of keen bronze made
In leafen shape.

    With stately stride
He crossed the level sands and wide,
Then on his shield the challenge gave—
His broad sword thund'ring like a wave—
For single combat.

    Red as gold
His locks upon his shoulders rolled;
A brazen helmet on his head
Flashed fire; his cheeks were white and red;
And all the Fians watched with awe
That hero young with knotted jaw,
Whose eyes, set deep, and blue and hard,
Surveyed their ranks with cold regard;
While his broad forehead, seamed with care,
Drooped shadowily: his eyebrows fair
Were sloping sideways o'er his eyes
With pondering o'er the mysteries.

The eyes of all the Fians sought
Heroic Groll, whose face was wrought
With lines of deep, perplexing thought—
For gazing on the valiant Conn,
He mourned that his own youth was gone,
When, strong and fierce and bold, he shed
The life-blood of the boastful Red,
Whom none save he would meet. He heard
The challenge, and nor spake, nor stirred,
Nor feared; but now grown old, when hate
And lust of glory satiate—
His heart took pride in Conn, and shared
The kinship of the brave.

    Who dared
To meet the Viking bold, if he
The succour of the band, should be
Found faltering or in despair?
Until that day the Fians ne'er
Of one man had such fear.

Elves and Heroes

   Old Goll
Sat musing on a grassy knoll,
They deemed he shared their dread ... Not so
Wise Finn, who spake forth firm and slow—
"Goll, son of Morna, peerless man,
The keen desire of every clan,
Far-famed for many a valiant deed,
Strong hero in the time of need.
I vaunt not Conn ... nor deem that thou
Dost falter, save with meekness, now—
But why shouldst thou not take the head
Of this bold youth, as of The Red,
His sire, in other days?"

   Goll spake—
"O noble Finn, for thy sweet sake
Mine arms I'd seize with ready hand,
Although to answer thy command
My blood to its last drop were spilled—
By Crom! were all the Fians killed,
My sword would never fail to be
A strong defence to succour thee."

Upon his hard right arm with haste
His crooked and pointed shield he braced,
He clutched his sword in his left hand—
While round that hero of the band
The Fian warriors pressed, and praised
His valour ... Mute was Goll ... They raised,
Smiting their hands, the battle-cry,
To urge him on to victory.

The one-eyed Goll went forth alone,
His face was like a mountain stone,—
Cold, hard, and grey; his deep-drawn breath
Came heavily, like a man nigh death—
But his firm mouth, with lips drawn thin,
Deep sunken in his wrinkled skin,
Was cunningly crooked; his hair was white,
On his bald forehead gleamed a bright
And livid scar that Conn's great sire
Had cloven when their swords struck fire—
Burly and dauntless, full of might,

Elves and Heroes

Old Goll went humbly forth to fight
With arrogant Conn ... It seemed The Red
In greater might was from the dead,
Restored in his fierce son ...

      A deep
Swift silence fell, like sudden sleep,
On all the Fians waiting there
In sharp suspense and half despair ...
The morn was still. A skylark hung
In mid-air flutt'ring, and sung
A lullaby that grew more sweet
Amid the stillness, in the heat
And splendour of the sun: the lisp
Of faint wind in the herbage crisp
Went past them; and around the bare
And foam-striped sand-banks gleaming fair,
The faintly-panting waves were cast
By the wan deep fatigued and vast.

O great was Conn in that dread hour,
And all the Fians feared his power,
And watched, as in a darksome dream,
The warriors meet ... They saw the gleam
Of swift, up-lifted swords, and then
A breathless moment came, as when
The lithe and living lightning's flash
Makes pause, until the thunder's crash
Is splintered through the air.

      Loud o'er
The blue sea and the shining shore
Broke forth the crash of arms ... The roll
Of Conn's fierce blows that baffled Goll
On sword and shield resounding rang,
While that old warrior stooped and sprang
Sideways, and swerved, or backward leapt,
As swiftly as the bronze blade swept
Above him and around ... He swayed,
Stumbling, but rose ... But, though his blade
Was ever nimble to defend,
The Fians feared the fight would end
In victory for Conn.

Elves and Heroes

       ... 'Twas like
As when an eagle swoops to strike,
But swerves with flutt'ring wings, as nigh
Its head a javelin gleams ... A cry
That banished fear of Conn's great blows
From out the Fian ranks arose,
As, like a plumed reed in a gust,
Goll suddenly stooped — a deadly thrust
That drew the first blood in the fray
He darting gave ... With quick dismay
The valiant Conn drew back ...

       Again
He leapt at Goll, but sought in vain
To blind him with his blows that fell
Like snowflakes on a sullen well —
For Goll was calm, while great Conn raged,
As hour by hour the conflict waged;
He was a blast-defying tree —
A crag that spurned a furious sea,
And all the Fians with one mind
Set firm their faith in Goll

       The wind
Rose like a startled bird from out
The heather at the huntsman's shout
In swift and blust'ring flight At noon
The sun rolled in a cloudy swoon
Dimly, and over the rolling deep
Gust followed gust with shadowy sweep;
And waves that streamed their snowy locks
Were tossing high against the rocks
Seaward, while round the sands ebbed wide
Scrambled the fierce devouring tide

O, Conn was like a hound at morn,
That springs upon an elk forlorn
Among the hills. He was a proud
Cascade that leaps a cliff with loud
Unspending fall So fierce, so fair
Was arrogant Conn, but Goll fought there
Keen-eyed, with ready guard, at bay —
He was as a boar in that fierce fray.

Elves and Heroes

The waves were humbled on the shore,
And silent fell, amid the roar
And crash of battle Mute and still
The Fians watched; while on the hill
The little elves came out and gazed,
To be amused and were amazed ...
They saw upon the shrinking sands
The warriors with restless hands
And busy blades, with shields that rose
To buffet the unceasing blows;
They saw before the rising flood
The flash of fire, the flash of blood;
And watched the men with panting breath,
Striving to be the slaves of death;
Now darting wide, now swerving round,
Now clashed together in a bound,
With splitting swords that smote so fast,
As hour by hour unheeded past.

The sands were torn and tossed like spray
Before the whirlwind of the fray,
That waged in fury till the sun
Sank, and the day's last loops were spun—
Then terrible was Goll ... He rose
A tempest of increasing blows,
More furious and fast, as dim,
Uncertain twilight fell ... More grim
And great he grew as, looming large,
He fought, and pressing to the marge
Of ocean, he o'erpowered and drave
The Viking hero back; till wave
O'er ready wave that hurried fleet,
Snuffled and snarled about their feet ...

Then with a mighty shout that made
The rocks around him ring, his blade
Swept like a flash of fire to smite
The last fell blow in that fierce fight—
So great Conn perished like The Red
By Goll's left hand ... his life-blood spread
Over the quenching sands where rolled
His head entwined with locks of gold.
Then passed like thunder o'er the sea

Elves and Heroes

The Fian shout of victory.
And, trembling on the tossing ships,
The Vikings heard, with voiceless lips
And dim, despairing eyes ... Alone
Stood Goll, and like a silent stone
Bulking upon a ben-side bare,
He bent above the hero fair—
Remembering the mighty Red,
And wondering that Conn lay dead.

[Footnote 1: May Day.]

[Footnote 2: Traditional Holy Hill]

THE SONG OF GOLL.

O Son of The Red,
Undone and laid dead—
  The blood of a hero
My cold blade hath shed.

Who fought me to-day?
Who sought me to slay?—
  The son of yon High King
I slew in the fray.

O blade that yon brave
Low laid in the grave,
  Ye gladdened the Fians
But grief to Conn gave.

Stone-hearted and strong,
Lone-hearted with long,
  Dark brooding, he sought to
Avenge his deep wrong.

Fair Son of The Red,
Care none thou art dead?—
  Old Goll of Clan Morna
Will mourn thou hast bled.

O where shall be found
To share with thee round
  The halls of Valhalla
Thy glory renowned?

O true as the blade
That slew thee, and made
  My fear and thine anger
For ever to fade—

Ah! when upon earth
Again will have birth
  A son of such honour
And bravery and worth?

Elves and Heroes

Above thee in splendour
A love that could render
　Brave service, burned star-like
And constant and tender.

With fearing my name,
With hearing my fame,
　O none would dare combat
With Goll till Conn came? ...

O great was thine ire—
The fate of thy sire,
　Awaiting thy coming,
Consumed thee like fire.

O Son of The Red,
Undone and laid dead—
　The blood of a hero
My cold blade hath shed.

Elves and Heroes

THE BLUE MEN OF THE MINCH.

When the tide is at the turning and the wind is fast asleep,
And not a wave is curling on the wide, blue Deep,
O the waters will be churning on the stream that never smiles,
Where the Blue Men are splashing round the charmèd isles.

As the summer wind goes droning o'er the sun-bright seas,
And the Minch is all a-dazzle to the Hebrides;
They will skim along like salmon—you can see their shoulders gleam,
And the flashing of their fingers in the Blue Men's Stream.

But when the blast is raving and the wild tide races,
The Blue Men ere breast-high with foam-grey faces;
They'll plunge along with fury while they sweep the spray behind,
O, they'll bellow o'er the billows and wail upon the wind.

And if my boat be storm-toss'd and beating for the bay,
They'll be howling and be growling as they drench it with their spray—
For they'd like to heel it over to their laughter when it lists,
Or crack the keel between them, or stave it with their fists.

O weary on the Blue Men, their anger and their wiles!
The whole day long, the whole night long, they're splashing round the
    isles;
They'll follow every fisher—ah! they'll haunt the fisher's dream—
When billows toss, O who would cross the Blue Men's Stream?

THE URISK.

O the night I met the Urisk on the wide, lone moor!
Ah! would I be forgetting of The Thing that came with me?
For it was big and black as black, and it was dour as dour,
It shrank and grew and had no shape of aught I e'er did see.

For it came creeping like a cloud that's moving all alone,
Without the sound of footsteps ... and I heard its heavy sighs ...
Its face was old and grey, and like a lichen-covered stone,
And its tangled locks were dropping o'er its sad and weary eyes.

O it's never the word it had to say in anger or in woe—
It would not seek to harm me that had never done it wrong,
As fleet—O like the deer!—I went, or I went panting slow,
The waesome thing came with me on that lonely road and long.

O eerie was the Urisk that convoy'd me o'er the moor!
When I was all so helpless and my heart was full of fear,
Nor when it was beside me or behind me was I sure—
I knew it would be following—I knew it would be near!

Elves and Heroes

THE NIMBLE MEN.

(AURORA BOREALIS.)

When Angus Ore, the wizard,
   His fearsome wand will raise,
The night is filled with splendour,
   And the north is all ablaze;
From clouds of raven blackness,
   Like flames that leap on high—
All merrily dance the Nimble Men across the Northern Sky.

Now come the Merry Maidens,
   All gowned in white and green,
While the bold and ruddy fellows
   Will be flitting in between—
O to hear the fairy piper
   Who will keep them tripping by!—
The men and maids who merrily dance across the Northern Sky.

O the weird and waesome music,
   And the never-faltering feet!
O their fast and strong embraces,
   And their kisses hot and sweet!
There's a lost and languished lover
   With a fierce and jealous eye,
As merrily flit the Nimble Folk across the Northern Sky.

So now the dance is over,
   And the dancers sink to rest—
There's a maid that has two lovers,
   And there's one she loves the best;
He will cast him down before her,
   She will raise him with a sigh—
Her love so bright who danced to-night across the Northern Sky.

Then up will leap the other,
   And up will leap his clan—
O the lover and his company
   Will fight them man to man—
All shrieking from the conflict

Elves and Heroes

    The merry maidens fly—
There's a Battle Royal raging now across the Northern Sky.

    Through all the hours of darkness
      The fearsome fight will last;
    They are leaping white with anger,
      And the blows are falling fast—
    And where the slain have tumbled
      A pool of blood will lie—
O it's dripping on the dark green stones from out the Northern Sky.

    When yon lady seeks her lover
      In the cold and pearly morn,
    She will find that he has fallen
      By the hand that she would scorn,—
    She will clasp her arms about him,
      And in her anguish die!—
O never again will trip the twain across the Northern Sky.

Elves and Heroes

MY GUNNA.

When my kine are on the hill,
Who will charm them from all ill?
While I'll sleep at ease until
  All the cocks are crowing clear.
Who'll be herding them for me?
It's the elf I fain would see—
For they're safe as safe can be
  When the Gunna will be near.

He will watch the long weird night,
When the stars will shake with fright,
Or the ghostly moon leaps bright
  O'er the ben like Beltane fire.
If my kine would seek the corn,
He will turn them by the horn—
And I'll find them all at morn
  Lowing sweet beside the byre.

Croumba's bard has second-sight,
And he'll moan the Gunna's plight,
When the frosts are flickering white,
  And the kine are housed till day;
For he'll see him perched alone
On a chilly old grey stone,
Nibbling, nibbling at a bone
  That we'll maybe throw away.

He's so hungry, he's so thin,
If he'd come we'd let him in,
For a rag of fox's skin
  Is the only thing he'll wear.
He'll be chittering in the cold
As he hovers round the fold,
With his locks of glimmering gold
  Twined about his shoulders bare.

Elves and Heroes

THE GRUAGACH.

(MILKMAID'S SONG.)

The lightsome lad wi' yellow hair,
The elfin lad that is so fair,
He comes in rich and braw attire—
To loose the kine within the byre—

   My lightsome lad, my leering lad,
    He's tittering here; he's tittering there—
   I'll hear him plain, but seek in vain
    To find my lad wi' yellow hair.

He's dressed so fine, he's dressed so grand,
A supple switch is in his hand;
I've seen while I a-milking sat
The shadow of his beaver hat.

   My lightsome lad, my leering lad,
    He's tittering here; he's tittering there—
   I'll hear him plain, but seek in vain
    To find my lad wi' yellow hair.

My chuckling lad, so full o' fun,
Around the corners he will run;
Behind the door he'll sometimes jink,
And blow to make my candle blink.

   My lightsome lad, my leering lad,
    He's tittering here; he's tittering there—
   I'll hear him plain, but seek in vain
    To find my lad wi' yellow hair.

The elfin lad that is so braw,
He'll sometimes hide among the straw;
He's sometimes leering from the loft—
He's tittering low and tripping soft.

   My lightsome lad, my leering lad,
    He's tittering here; he's tittering there—

Elves and Heroes

I'll hear him plain, but seek in vain
   To find my lad wi' yellow hair.

And every time I'll milk the kine
He'll have his share—the luck be mine!
I'll pour it in yon hollowed stone,
He'll sup it when he's all alone—

   My lightsome lad, my leering lad,
      He's tittering here; he's tittering there—
   I'll hear him plain, but seek in vain
      To find my lad wi' yellow hair.

O me! if I'd his milk forget,
Nor cream, nor butter I would get;
Ye needna' tell—I ken full well—
On all my kine he'd cast his spell.

   My lightsome lad, my leering lad,
      He's tittering here; he's tittering there—
   I'll hear him plain, but seek in vain
      To find my lad wi' yellow hair.

On nights when I would rest at ease,
The merry lad begins to tease;
He'll loose the kine to take me out,
And titter while I move about.

   My lightsome lad, my leering lad,
      He's tittering here; he's tittering there—
   I'll hear him plain, but seek in vain
      To find my lad wi' yellow hair.

Elves and Heroes

THE LITTLE OLD MAN OF THE BARN.

When all the big lads will be hunting the deer,
And no one for helping Old Callum comes near,
O who will be busy at threshing his corn?
Who will come in the night and be going at morn?

   The Little Old Man of the Barn,
   Yon Little Old Man—
   A bodach forlorn will be threshing his corn,
   The Little Old Man of the Barn.

When the peat will turn grey and the shadows fall deep,
And weary Old Callum is snoring asleep;
When yon plant by the door will keep fairies away,
And the horse-shoe sets witches a-wandering till day.

   The Little Old Man of the Barn,
   Yon Little Old Man—
   Will thresh with no light in the mouth of the night,
   The Little Old Man of the Barn.

For the bodach is strong though his hair is so grey,
He will never be weary when he goes away—
The bodach is wise—he's so wise, he's so dear—
When the lads are all gone, he will ever be near.

   The Little Old Man of the Barn,
   Yon Little Old Man—
   So tight and so braw he will bundle the straw—
   The Little Old Man of the Barn.

YON FAIRY DOG.

'Twas bold MacCodrum of the Seals,
  Whose heart would never fail,
Would hear yon fairy ban-dog fierce
  Come howling down the gale;
The patt'ring of the paws would sound
Like horse's hoofs on frozen ground,
While o'er its back and curling round
  Uprose its fearsome tail.

'Twas bold MacCodrum of the Seals—
  Yon man that hath no fears—
Beheld the dog with dark-green back
  That bends not when it rears;
Its sides were blacker than the night,
But underneath the hair was white;
Its paws were yellow, its eyes were bright,
  And blood-red were its ears.

'Twas bold MacCodrum of the Seals—
  The man who naught will dread—
Would wait it, stooping with his spear,
  As nigh to him it sped;
The big black head it turn'd and toss'd,
"I'll strike," cried he, "ere I'll be lost,"
For every living thing that cross'd
  Its path would tumble dead.

'Twas bold MacCodrum of the Seals—
  The man who ne'er took fright—
Would watch it bounding from the hills
  And o'er the moors in flight.
When it would leave the Uist shore,
Across the Minch he heard it roar—
Like yon black cloud it bounded o'er
  The Coolin Hills that night.

Elves and Heroes

THE WATER-HORSE.

O the Water-Horse will come over the heath,
  With the foaming mouth and the flashing eyes,
He's black above and he's white beneath—
  The hills are hearing the awesome cries;
The sand lies thick in his dripping hair,
And his hoofs are twined with weeds and ware.

Alas! for the man who would clutch the mane—
  There's no spell to help and no charm to save!
Who rides him will never return again,
  Were he as strong, O were he as brave
As Fin-mac-Coul, of whom they'll tell—
He thrashed the devil and made him yell.

He'll gallop so fierce, he'll gallop so fast,
  So high he'll rear, and so swift he'll bound—
Like the lightning flash he'll go prancing past,
  Like the thunder-roll will his hoofs resound—
And the man perchance who sees and hears,
He would blind his eyes, he would close his ears.

The horse will bellow, the horse will snort,
  And the gasping rider will pant for breath—
Let the way be long, or the way be short,
  It will have one end, and the end is death;
In yon black loch, from off the shore,
The horse will splash, and be seen no more.

THE CHANGELING.

By night they came and from my bed
  They stole my babe, and left behind
A thing I hate, a thing I dread—
  A changeling who is old and blind;
He's moaning all the night and day
For those who took my babe away.

My little babe was sweet and fair,
  He crooned to sleep upon my breast—
But O the burden I must bear!
  This drinks all day and will not rest—
My little babe had hair so light—
And his is growing dark as night.

Yon evil day when I would leave
  My little babe the stook behind!—
The fairies coming home at eve
  Upon an eddy of the wind,
Would cast their eyes with envy deep
Upon my heart's-love in his sleep.

What holy woman will ye find
  To weave a spell and work a charm?
A holy woman, pure and kind,
  Who'll keep my little babe from harm—
Who'll make the evil changeling flee,
And bring my sweet one back to me?

Elves and Heroes

MY FAIRY LOVER.

My fairy lover, my fairy lover,
  My fair, my rare one, come back to me—
All night I'm sighing, for thee I'm crying,
  I would be dying, my love, for thee.

Thine eyes were glowing like blue-bells blowing,
  With dew-drops twinkling their silvery fires;
Thine heart was panting with love enchanting,
  For mine was granting its fond desires.

  My fairy lover, my fairy lover,
    My fair, my rare one, come back to me—
  All night I'm sighing, for thee I'm crying,
    I would be dying, my love, for thee.

Thy brow had brightness and lily-whiteness,
  Thy cheeks were clear as yon crimson sea;
Like broom-buds gleaming, thy locks were streaming,
  As I lay dreaming, my love, of thee.

  My fairy lover, my fairy lover,
    My fair, my rare one, come back to me—
  All night I'm sighing, for thee I'm crying,
    I would be dying, my love, for thee.

Thy lips that often with love would soften,
  They beamed like blooms for the honey-bee;
Thy voice came ringing like some bird singing
  When thou wert bringing thy gifts to me.

  My fairy lover, my fairy lover,
    My fair, my rare one, come back to me—
  All night I'm sighing, for thee I'm crying,
    I would be dying, my love, for thee.

O thou'rt forgetting the hours we met in
  The Vale of Tears at the even-tide,
Or thou'd come near me to love and cheer me,
  And whisper clearly, "O be my bride!"

Elves and Heroes

My fairy lover, my fairy lover,
  My fair, my rare one, come back to me—
All night I'm sighing, for thee I'm crying,
  I would be dying, my love, for thee.

What spell can bind thee? I search to find thee
  Around the knoll that thy home would be—
Where thou did'st hover, my fairy lover,
  The clods will cover and comfort me.

My fairy lover, my fairy lover,
  My fair, my rare one, come back to me—
All night I'm sighing, on thee I'm crying,
  I would be dying, my love, for thee.

Elves and Heroes

THE FIANS OF KNOCKFARREL.

(A Ross-shire Legend.)

I.

On steep Knockfarrel had the Fians made,
For safe retreat, a high and strong stockade
Around their dwellings. And when winter fell
And o'er Strathpeffer laid its barren spell —
When days were bleak with storm, and nights were drear
And dark and lonesome, well they loved to hear
The songs of Ossian, peerless and sublime —
Their blind, grey bard, grown old before his time,
Lamenting for his son — the young, the brave
Oscar, who fell beside the western wave
In Gavra's bloody and unequal fight.

Round Ossian would they gather in the night,
Beseeching him for song ... And when he took
His clarsach, from the magic strings he shook
A maze of trembling music, falling sweet
As mossy waters in the summer heat;
And soft as fainting moor-winds when they leave
The fume of myrtle, on a dewy eve,
Bound flush'd and teeming tarns that all night hear
Low elfin pipings in the woodlands near.

'Twas thus he sang of love, and in a dream
The fair maids sighed to hear. But when his theme
Was the long chase that Finn and all his men
Followed with lightsome heart from glen to glen —
His song was free as morn, and clear and loud
As skylarks carolling below a cloud
In sweet June weather ... And they heard the fall
Of mountain streams, the huntsman's windy call
Across the heaving hills, the baying hound
Among the rocks, while echoes answered round —
They heard, and shared the gladness of the chase.

He sang the glories of the Fian race,

Elves and Heroes

Whose fame is flashed through Alba far and wide—
Their valorous deeds he sang with joy and pride ...
When their dark foemen from the west came o'er
The ragged hills, and when on Croumba's shore
The Viking hordes descending, fought and fled—
And when brave Conn, who would avenge the Red,
By one-eyed Goll was slain. Of Finn he sang,
And Dermaid, while the clash of conflict rang
In billowy music through the heroes' hall—
And many a Fian gave the battle-call
When Ossian sang.

    Haggard and old, with slow
And falt'ring steps, went Winter through the snow,
As if its dreary round would ne'er be done—
The last long winter of their days—begun
Ere yet the latest flush of falling leaves
Had faded in the breath of chilling eves;
Nor ended in the days of longer light,
When dawn and eve encroached upon the night—
A weary time it was! The long Strath lay
Snow-wreathed and pathless, and from day to day
The tempests raved across the low'ring skies,
And they grew weak and pale, with hollow eyes,
The while their stores shrank low, waiting the dawn
Of that sweet season when through woodlands wan
Fresh flowers flutter and the wild birds sing—
For Winter on the forelock of the Spring
Its icy fingers laid. The huntsmen pined
In their dim dwellings, wearily confined,
While the loud, hungry tempest held its sway—
The red-eyed wolves grew bold and came by day,
And birds fell frozen in the snow.

    Then through
The trackless Strath a balmy south wind blew
To usher lusty Spring. Lo! in a night
The snows 'gan shrinking upon plain and height,
And morning broke in brightness to the sound
Of falling waters, while a peace profound
Possessed the world around them, and the blue
Bared heaven above ... Then all the Fians knew
That Winter's spell was broken, and each one

Elves and Heroes

Made glad obeisance to the golden sun.

Three days around Knockfarrel they pursued
The chase across the hills and through the wood,
Round Ussie Loch and Dingwall's soundless shore;
But meagre were the burdens that they bore
At even to their dwellings. To the west
"But sorrow not," said Finn, when all dismay'd
They hastened on a drear and bootless quest—
With weary steps they turned to their stockade,
"To-morrow will we hunt towards the east
To high Dunskaith, and then make gladsome feast
By night when we return."

        Or ever morn
Had broken, Finn arose, and on his horn
Blew loud the huntsman's blast that round the ben
Was echoed o'er and o'er ... Then all his men
Gathered about him in the dusk, nor knew
What dim forebodings filled his heart and drew
His brows in furrowed care. His eyes a-gleam
Still stared upon the horrors of a dream
Of evil omen that in vain he sought
To solve ... His voice came faint from battling thought,
As he to Garry spake—"Be thou the ward
Strong son of Morna: who, like thee, can guard
Our women from all peril!" ... Garry turned
From Finn in sullen silence, for he yearned
To join the chase once more. In stature he
Was least of all the tribe, but none could be
More fierce in conflict, fighting in the van,
Than that grim, wolfish, and misshapen man!

Then Finn to Caoilte spake, and gave command
To hasten forth before the Fian band—
The King of Scouts was he! And like the deer
He sped to find if foemen had come near—
Fierce, swarthy hillmen, waiting at the fords
For combat eager, or red Viking hordes
From out the Northern isles ... In Alba wide
No runner could keep pace by Caoilte's side,
And ere the Fians, following in his path,
Had wended from the deep and dusky strath,

Elves and Heroes

He swept o'er Clyne, and heard the awesome owls
That hoot afar and near in woody Foulis,
And he had reached the slopes of fair Rosskeen
Ere Finn by Fyrish came.

       The dawn broke green—
For the high huntsman of the morn had flung
His mantle o'er his back: stooping, he strung
His silver bow; then rising, bright and bold,
He shot a burning arrow of pure gold
That rent the heart of Night.

       As far behind
The Fians followed, Caoilte, like the wind,
Sped on—yon son of Ronan—o'er the wide
And marshy moor, and 'thwart the mountain side,—
By Delny's shore far-ebbed, and wan, and brown,
And through the woods of beautous Balnagown:
The roaring streams he vaulted on his spear,
And foaming torrents leapt, as he drew near
The sandy slopes of Nigg. He climbed and ran
Till high above Dunskaith he stood to scan
The outer ocean for the Viking ships,
Peering below his hand, with panting lips
A-gape, but wide and empty lay the sea
Beyond the barrier crags of Cromarty,
To the far sky-line lying blue and bare—
For no red pirate sought as yet to dare
The gloomy hazards of the fitful seas,
The gusty terrors, and the treacheries
Of fickle April and its changing skies—
And while he scanned the waves with curious eyes,
The sea-wind in his nostrils, who had spent
A long, bleak winter in Knockfarrel pent
Over the snow-wreathed Strath and buried wood,
A sense of freedom tingled in his blood—
The large life of the Ocean, heaving wide,
His heart possessed with gladness and with pride,
And he rejoiced to be alive.... Once more
He heard the drenching waves on that rough shore
Raking the shingles, and the sea-worn rocks
Sucking the brine through bared and lapping locks
Of bright, brown tangle; while the shelving ledges

Elves and Heroes

Poured back the swirling waters o'er their edges;
And billows breaking on a precipice
In spouts of spray, fell spreading like a fleece.

Sullen and sunken lay the reef, with sleek
And foaming lips, before the flooded creek
Deep-bunched with arrowy weed, its green expanse
Wind-wrinkled and translucent ... A bright trance
Of sun-flung splendour lay athwart the wide
Blue ocean swept with loops of silvern tide
Heavily heaving in a long, slow swell.

A lonely fisher in his coracle
Came round a headland, lifted on a wave
That bore him through the shallows to his cave,
Nor other being he saw.

   The birds that flew
Clamorous about the cliffs, and diving drew
Their prey from bounteous waters, on him cast
Cold, beady eyes of wonder, wheeling past
And sliding down the wind.

   II.

   The warm sun shone
On blind, grey Ossian musing all alone
Upon a knoll before the high stockade,
When Oscar's son came nigh. His hand he laid
On the boy's curls, and then his fingers strayed
Over the face and round the tender chin—
"Be thou as brave as Oscar, wise as Finn,"
Said Ossian, with a sigh. "Nay, I would be
A bard," the boy made answer, "like to thee."
"Alas! my son," the gentle Ossian said,
"My song was born in sorrow for the dead!...
O may such grief as Ossian's ne'er be thine!—
If thou would'st sing, may thou below the pine
Murmuring, thy dreams conceive, and happy be,
Nor hear but sorrow in the breaking sea
And death-sighs in the gale. Alas! my song
That rose in sorrow must survive in wrong—
My life is spent and vain—a day of thine

Elves and Heroes

Were better than a long, dark year of mine....
But come, my son—so lead me by the hand—
To hear the sweetest harper in the land—
The wild, free wind of Spring; all o'er the hills
And under, let us go, by tuneful rills
We'll wander, and my heart shall sweetened be
With echoes of the moorland melody—
My clarsach wilt thou bear." And so went they
Together from Knockfarrel. Long they lay
Within the woods of Brahan, and by the shore
Of silvery Conon wended, crossing o'er
The ford at Achilty, where Ossian told
The tale of Finn, who there had slain the bold
Black Arky in his youth. And ere the tale
Was ended, they had crossed to Tarradale.
Where dwelt a daughter of an ancient race
Deep-learned in lore, and with the gift to trace
The thread of life in the dark web of fate.
And she to Ossian cried, "Thou comest late
Too late, alas! this day of all dark days—
Knockfarrel is before me all ablaze—
A fearsome vision flaming to mine eyes—
O beating heart that bleeds! I hear the cries
Of those that perish in yon high stockade—
O many a tender lad, and lonesome maid,
Sweet wife and sleeping babe, and hero old—
O Ossian could'st thou see—O child, behold
Yon ruddy, closing clouds ... so falls the fate
Of all the tribe ... Alas! thou comest late." ...

III.

When Ossian from Knockfarrel went, a band
Of merry maidens, trooping hand in hand,
Came forth, with laughing eyes and flowing hair,
To share the freedom of the morning air;
Adown the steep they went, and through the wood
Where Garry splintered logs in sullen mood—
Pining to join the chase! His wrath he wrought
Upon the trees that morn, as if he fought
Against a hundred foemen from the west,
Till he grew weary, and was fain to rest.

Elves and Heroes

The maids were wont to shower upon his head
Their merry taunts, and oft from them he fled;
For of their quips and jests he had more fear
Than e'er he felt before a foeman's spear —
And so he chose to be alone.

        The air
Was heavily laden with the odour rare
Of deep, wind-shaken fir trees, breathing sweet,
As through the wood, the maids, with silent feet,
Went treading needled sward, in light and shade,
Now bright, now dim, like flow'rs that gleam and fade,
And ever bloom and ever pass away ...

Upon a fairy hillock Garry lay
In sunshine fast asleep: his head was bare,
And the wind rippling through his golden hair
Laid out the seven locks that were his pride,
Which one by one the maids securely tied
To tether-pins, while Garry, breathing deep,
Moaned low, and moved about in troubled sleep
Then to a thicket all the maidens crept,
And raised the Call of Warning ... Garry leapt
From dreams that boded ill, with sudden fear
That a fierce band of foemen had come near —
The seven fetters of his golden hair
He wrenched off as he leapt, and so laid bare
A shredded scalp of ruddy wounds that bled
With bitter agony ... The maidens fled
With laughter through the wood, and climb'd the path
Of steep Knockfarrel. Fierce was Garry's wrath
When he perceived who wronged him. With a shriek
That raised the eagles from the mountain peak,
He shook his spear, and ran with stumbling feet,
And sought for vengeance, speedy and complete —
The lust of blood possessed him, and he swore
To slay them.... But they shut the oaken door
Ere he had reached that high and strong stockade —
From whence, alas! nor wife, nor child, nor maid
Came forth again.

Elves and Heroes

IV.

      Soft-couch'd upon a bank
Lay Caoilte on the cliff-top, while he drank
The sweetness of the morning air, that brought
A spell of dreamful ease and pleasant thought,
With mem'ries from the deeps of other years
When Dermaid, unforgotten by his peers,
And Oscar, fair and young, went forth with mirth
A-hunting o'er the hills around the firth
On such an April morn....

      He leapt to hear
The Fians shouting from a woodland near
Their hunting-call. Then swift he sped a-pace,
With bounding heart, to join the gladsome chase;
Stooping he ran, with poised, uplifted spear,
As through the woods approached the nimble deer
That swerved, beholding him. With startled toss
Of antlers, down the slope it fled, to cross
The open vale before him ... To the west
The Fians, merging from the woodland, pressed
To head it shoreward ... All the fierce hounds bayed
With hungry ardour, and the deer, dismayed,
With foaming nostrils leapt, and strove to flee
Towards the deep, dark woods of Calrossie.
But Caoilte, fresh from resting, was more fleet
Than deer or dogs, and sped with naked feet,
Until upon a loose and sandy bank,
Plunging his spear into the smoking flank,
Its flight he stayed.... He stabbed it as it sank,
The life-blood spurting; and he saw it die
Or ever dog or huntsman had come nigh.

Then eager feast they made; and after long
And frequent fast of winter, they grew strong
As they had been of old. And of their fare
The lean and scrambling hounds had ready share.

Nor over-fed they in their merry mood,
But set to hunt again, and through the wood
Scattered with eager pace, ere yet the sun
Had climbed to highest noon; for lo! each one

Elves and Heroes

Had mem'ry of the famished cheeks and white
Of those who waited their return by night,
In steep Knockfarrel's desolate stockade—
O' many a beauteous and bethrothèd maid,
And mothers nursing babes, and warriors lying
In winter-fever's spell, the old men dying,
And slim, fair lads who waited to acclaim,
With gladsome shout, the huntsmen when they came
With burdens of the chase ... So they pursued
The hunt till eve was nigh. In Geanies wood
Another deer they slew ...

      Caoilte, who stood
On a high ridge alone ... with eager eyes
Scanning the prospect wide ... in mute surprise
Saw rising o'er Knockfarrel, a dark cloud
Of thick and writhing smoke ... Then fierce and loud
Upon his horn he blew the warning blast—
From out the woods the Fians hastened fast—
Lo! when they stared towards the western sky,
They saw their winter dwelling blazing high.

Then fear possessed them for their own, and grief
Unutterable. And thus spake their wise chief,
To whom came knowledge and the swift, sure thought—
"Alas! alas! an enemy hath wrought
Black vengeance on our kind. In yonder gleam
Of fearsome flame, the horrors of my dream
Are now accomplished—all we loved and cherished,
And sought, and fought for, in that pyre have perished!"

White-lipped they heard.... Then, wailing loud, they ran,
Following the nimble Caoilte, man by man,
Towards Knockfarrel; leaping on their spears
O'er marsh and stream. MacReithin, blind with tears,
Tumbled or leapt into a swollen flood
That swept him to the sea. But no man stood
To help or mourn him, for the eve grew dim—
And some there were, indeed, who envied him.

Elves and Heroes

V.

As snarls the wolf at bay within the wood
On huntsmen and their hounds, so Garry stood
Raging before the women who had made
Secure retreat within the high stockade;
He cursed them all, and their loud laughter rang
More bitter to his heart than e'en the pang
Of his fierce wounds. Then while his streaming blood
Half-blinded him, he hastened to the wood,
And a small tree upon his shoulders bore,
And fixed it fast against the oaken door,
That none might issue forth.

   Then once again
Towards the wood he turned, but all in vain
The women waited his return, till they
Grey weary.. for in pain and wrath he lay
In a close thicket, brooding o'er his shame,
And panting for revenge.

   Then Finn's wife came
To set the women to the wheel and loom,
With angry chiding; and a heavy gloom
Fell on them all. "Who knoweth," thus she spake,
"What evil may the Fian men o'ertake
This day of evil omens. Yester-night
I say the pale ghost of my sire with white
And trembling lips ... At morn before my sight
A raven darted from the wood, and slew
A brooding dove ... What fear is mine!... for who
Would us defend if our fierce foemen came—
When Garry is against us ... Much I blame
Thy wanton deed." ... The women heard in shame,
Nor answer made.

   The sun, with fiery gleam,
Scattered the feath'ry clouds, as in a dream
The spirits of the dead are softly swept
From severed visions sweet. A low wind crept
Around with falt'ring steps, and, pausing, sighed—
Then fled to murmur from the mountain side
Amid the pine-tree shade; while all aglow

Elves and Heroes

Ben-Wyvis bared a crest of shining snow
In barren splendour o'er the slumbering strath;
While some sat trembling, fearing Garry's wrath,
Some feared the coming of the foe, and some
Had vague forebodings, and were brooding dumb,
And longed to greet the huntsmen. Mothers laid
Their babes to sleep, and many a gentle maid
Sighed for her lover in that lone stockade;
And one who sat apart, with pensive eye,
Thus sang to hear the peewee's plaintive cry—

> *Peewee, peewee, crying sweet,*
>   *Crying early, crying late—*
> *Will your voice be never weary*
>   *Crying for your mate?*
> *Other hearts than thine are lonely,*
>   *Other hearts must wait.*
>
> *Peewee, peewee, I'd be flying*
>   *O'er the hills and o'er the sea,*
> *Till I found the love I long for*
>   *Whereso'er he'd be—*
> *Peewee crying, I'd be flying,*
>   *Could I fly like thee!*

When Garry, who had stanched his wounds, arose,
He seized his axe, and 'gan with rapid blows
To fell down fir trees. Through the silent strath
The hollow echoes rang. With fiendish wrath
He made resolve to heap the splintered wood
Against the door, and burn the hated brood
Of his tormentors one and all. He hewed
An ample pyre, then piled it thick and high,
While the sun, sloping to the western sky,
Proclaimed the closing of that fateful day.
But the doomed women little dreamed that they
Would have such fearsome end ... As Garry lay
Rubbing the firesticks till they 'gan to glow,
He heard a Fian mother singing low—

> *Sleep, O sleep, I'll sing to thee—*
>   *Moolachie, O moolachie.*
> *Sleep, O sleep, like yon grey stone,*

Elves and Heroes

Moolachie, mine own.

Sleep, O sleep, nor sigh nor fret ye,
  And the goblins will not get ye,
I will shield ye, I will pet ye —
  Moolachie, mine own.

The mother sang, the gentle babe made moan —
And Garry heard them with a heart of stone ...
With fiendish laugh, he saw the leaping flames
Possess the pyre; he heard the shrieking dames,
And maids and children, wailing in the gloom
Of smothering smoke, e'er they had met their doom.
Then when the high stockade was blazing red,
Ere yet their cries were silenced, Garry fled,
And westward o'er the shouldering hills he sped.

VI.

A broad, faint twilight lingered to unfold
The sun's slow-dying beams of tangled gold,
And the long, billowy hills, in gathering shade,
Their naked peaks and ebon crags displayed
Sharp-rimmed against the tender heaven and pale;
And misty shadows gathered in the vale —
When Caoilte to Knockfarrel came, and saw
Amid the dusk, with sorrow and with awe,
The ruins of their winter dwelling laid
In smouldering ashes; while the high stockade
Around the rocky wall, like ragged teeth,
Was crackling o'er the melting stones beneath,
Still darting flame, and flickering in the breeze.

He sped towards the wood, and through the trees
Called loud for those who perished. On his fair
And gentle spouse he called in his despair.
His sweet son, and his sire, whose hair was white
As Wyvis snow, he called for in the night.
Full loud and long across the Strath he cried —
The echoes mocked him from the mountain side.

Ah! when his last hope faded like the wave
Of twilight ebbing o'er the hills, he gave

Elves and Heroes

His heart to utter grief and deep despair;
And the cold stars peer'd down with pitiless stare,
While sank the wind in silence on its flight
Through the dark hollows of the spacious night;
And distant sounds seem'd near. In his dismay
He heard a Fian calling far away.
The night-bird answered back with dismal cry,
Like to a wounded man about to die —
But Caoilte's lips were silent ... Once again
And nearer, came the voice that cried in vain.
Then swift steps climbed Knockfarrel's barren steep,
And Alvin called, with trembling voice and deep,
To Caoilte, crouching low, with bended head,
"Who liveth?" ... "I am here alone," he said ...
Thus Fian after Fian came to share
Their bitter grief, in silence and despair.

All night they kept lone watch, until the dawn
With stealthy fingers o'er the east had drawn
Its dewy veil and dim. Then Finn arose
From deep and sleepless brooding o'er his woes,
And spake unto the Fians, "Who shall rest
While flees our evil foeman farther west?
Arise!" ... "But who hath done this deed?" they sighed;
And Finn made answer, "Garry." ... Then they cried
For vengeance swift and terrible, and leapt
To answer Finn's command.

          A cold wind swept
From out the gates of morning, moaning loud,
As swift they hastened forth. A ragged shroud
Of gathering tempest o'er Ben-Wyvis cast
A sudden gloom, and round it, falling fast,
It drifted o'er the darkened slopes and bare,
And snow-flakes swirled in the chill morning air —
Then o'er the sea, the sun leapt large and bright,
Scatt'ring the storm. And moor and crag lay white,
As westward o'er the hills the Fians all
In quest of Garry sped.

          At even-fall
They found him ... On the bald and rocky side
Of steep Scour-Vullin, Garry lay to hide

Elves and Heroes

Within a cave, which, backward o'er the snow,
He entered, that his steps might seem to show
He had fled eastward by the path he came.
All day he sought to flee them in his shame,
Watching from lofty crag or deep ravine,
And crouching in the heath, with haggard mien—
He sought in vain to hide till darkness cast
Its blinding cloak betwixt them.

                When at last
Finn cried, "Come forth, thou dog of evil deeds,
Nor respite seek!" ... His limbs like wind-swept reeds
Trembled and bent beneath him; so he rose
And came to meet his friends who were his foes—
Then unto Finn he spake with accents meek,
"One last request I of the Fians seek,
Whom I have loved in peace and served in strife"—
"'Tis thine," said Finn, "but ask not for thy life,
For thou art 'mong the Fians." ... "I would die,"
Said Garry, "with my head laid on thy thigh;
And let young Alvin take thy sword, that he
May give the death that will mine honour be."

'Twas so he lay to die ... But as the blade
Swept bright, young Alvin, keen for vengeance, swayed,
And slipped upon the sward ... And his fierce blow
That Garry slew, the Fian chief laid low—
A grievous wound was gaping on his thigh,
And poured his life-blood forth ... A low, weird cry
The great Finn gave, as he fell back and swooned—
In vain they strove to stanch the fearsome wound—
His life ebbed slowly with the sun's last ray
In gathering gloom ... And when in death he lay,
The glory of the Fians passed away.

Elves and Heroes

HER EVIL EYE.

O Mairi Dhu, the weaver's wife,
  Will have the evil eye;
The fear will come about my heart
  When she'll be passing by;
She'll have the piercing look to wound
  The very birds that fly.

I would not have her evil wish,
  I would not have her praise,
For like the shadow would her curse,
  Me follow all my days—
When she my churning will speak well,
  No butter can I raise.

O Mairi Dhu will have the eye
  To wound the very deer—
Ah! would she scowl upon my bairns
  When her they would come near?
They'll have the red cords round their necks,
  So they'll have naught to fear.

It's Murdo Ban, the luckless man,
  Against her would prevail;
And first her eye was on his churn,
  Then on the milking pail;
When she would praise the brindled cow,
  The cow began to ail.

The trout that gambol in the pool
  She'll wound when she goes past;
Then weariness will come upon
  The fins that flicked so fast;
And one by one the lifeless things
  Will on the stones be cast.

O Mairi Dhu, you gave yon sprain
  To poor Dun Para's arm;
It is myself would have the work
  Undoing of the harm—

Elves and Heroes

I'd twist around the three-ply cord
  Well-knotted o'er the charm.

Your eye you'd put on yon sweet babe
  O' Lachlan o' Loch-Glass;
He'd fill the wooden ladle where
  The dead and living pass—
And with the water, silver-charmed,
  He'd save his little lass.

I'll lock my cheese within the chest,
  My butter I will hide;
I'll bar the byre at milking time,
  Although you'll wait outside—
You'll maybe go another way—
  Who'll care for you to bide?

Elves and Heroes

A CURSING

So you're coming, ye reivers and rogues,
  When the men will be fighting afar—
Oh! all the Mac Quithens[1] are bold
  When it's only with women they'll war

Weasels that creep in the dark!
  Foxes that prowl in the night!
Rats that are hated and vile!—
  O hasten you out of my sight!

Oh! my cow you would take from my byre?—
  This day will the beggars be brave!
You'd be lifting the thatch from the roof
  If you hadna' a roof to your cave

Your chief he's the lord o' the lies!
  A wind-bag his wife wi' the brag!
Your clan is the pride o' the thieves—
  Whose meal will you have in your bag?

Now, Laspuig Maclan[2] may blush—
  Oh! he'll be the sorrowful man—
His fame for the thieving is gone
  To the reivers and rogues of your clan

You'll spare me "so old and so frail,
  Fitter to die than to live?"
But maybe I'll slay with the tongue
  And the heart that will never forgive

The curse of the frail will be strong,
  The curse of the widow be sure;
O the curse of the wrong'd will avenge,
  Black, black is the curse of the poor!

Ha! laugh at your ease while you can—
  Laugh! it's the devil's turn next—
For after I'm done with you all,
  O who will be doleful and vext?

Elves and Heroes

Bare-kneed on the ground will I go—
  My hair on my shoulders let fall,
Now hear me and never forget
  My curses I'll cast on you all

Little increase to your clan!
  The down-mouth to you and to yours!
The blight on your little black cave!
  The luck o' a Friday on moors!

Fire upon land be your lot!
  Drowning in storm on the deep!
Leave not a son to succeed!
  Leave not a daughter to weep!

Here's the bad meeting to you!
  Death without priest be your fate!
Go to your grandfather's[3] house—
  The Son of the Cursing[4] will wait!

[Footnote 1: This clan, which had an evil reputation, is extinct]

[Footnote 2: Laspuig MacIan—A famous thief]

[Footnote 3: "Grandfather's house"—The grave]

[Footnote 4: "Son of the Cursing"—The devil]

LEOBAG'S[1] WARNING.

Would Murdo make the wry mouth?
  Is Ailie cross-eyed?
O mock no more the beggar man,
  You'll scorn wi' pride!
The wind that will be blowing west,
  Might turn and blow south—
O, Ailie, it would fix your eyes
  And Murdo's wry mouth.

O mind ye o' the Leobag
  And yon rock cod—
"Ho! there's the mouth," the 'cute one cried,
  "For the hook and rod!"
The tide it would be turning while
  The Leobag would mock—
And that is why it's gaping as
  It gaped below the rock.

[Footnote 1: Leobag—The flounder.]

TOBER MHUIRE.

(WELL OF ST MARY.)

'Tis for thee I will be pining,
  Tober Mhuire.
Thou art deep and sweet and shining,
  Tober Mhuire.
In the dimness I'll be dying,
And my soul for thee is sighing
With the blessings on thee lying—
  Tober Mhuire.

O thy cool, sweet waters dripping,
  Tober Mhuire,
Now my sere lips would be sipping,
  Tober Mhuire.
O my lips are sere and burning—
For thy waters I'll be yearning,
And yon road of no returning,
  Tober Mhuire.

O thy coolness and thy sweetness,
  Tober Mhuire.
O thy sureness and completeness,
  Tober Mhuire.
O this life I would be leaving,
With the greyness of its grieving,
And the deeps of its deceiving,
  Tober Mhuire.

I would sip thy waters holy,
  Tober Mhuire.
While the drops of life drip slowly,
  Tober Mhuire—
Till the wings of angel whiteness,
With their softness and their lightness,
Blind me, fold me, in their brightness—
  Tober Mhuire.

SLEEPY SONG.

(Sung by Grainne to Diarmid in their Flight from the Fians.)

Sleep a little O Diarmid, Diarmid,
   Sleep in the deep lone cave;
Sleep a little—a little little,
   Love whom my love I gave—
Wearily falls O Diarmid, Diarmid,
   Wearily falls the wave.

Sleep a little, O Diarmid, Diarmid,
   Sleep, and have never a fear;
Sleep a little—a little little,
   Love whom I love so dear—
A weary wind, O Diarmid, Diarmid,
   A weary wind I hear.

Sleep a little, O Diarmid, Diarmid,
   Sleep, while I watch till you wake;
Sleep a little—a little little,
   Love whom I'll ne'er forsake—
Sleep a little, and blessings on you
   My lamb, or my heart will break.

SONG OF THE SEA.

The sea sings loud, the sea sings low,
And sweet is the chime of its ebb and flow
   Over the shingly strand;
For its strange, sweet song that woos my ear
The first man heard, as the last shall hear—
   Seeking to understand ...

Elves and Heroes

THE DEATH OF CUCHULLIN.

Now when the last hour of his life drew nigh,
Cuchullin woke from dreams forewarning death;
And cold and awesome came the night-bird's cry —
An evil omen the magician saith —
A low gust panted like a man's last breath,
As morning crept into the chamber black;
Then all his weapons clashed and tumbled from the rack.

For the last time his evil foemen came;
The sons of Calatin by Lugaid led.
The land lay smouldering with smoke and flame;
The duns were fallen and the fords ran red;
And widows fled, lamenting for their dead,
To fair Emania on that fateful day,
Where all forsworn with fighting great Cuchullin lay.

Levarchan, whom he loved, a maid most fair,
Rose-lipp'd, with yellow hair and sea-grey eyes,
The evil tidings to Cuchullin bare.
And, trembling in her beauty, bade him rise;
Niamh, brave Conal's queen, the old, the wise,
Urged him with clamour of the land's alarms,
And, stirr'd with vengeful might, the hero sprang to arms.

His purple mantle o'er his shoulders wide
In haste he flung, and tow'ring o'er them stood
All scarr'd and terrible in battle pride —
His brooch, that clasp'd his mantle and his hood
Then fell his foot to pierce, and his red blood
Follow'd, like fate, behind him as he stepp'd
Levarchan shriek'd, and Niamh moaned his doom and wept

Thus sallying forth he called his charioteer,
And bade him yoke the war-steeds of his choice —
The Grey of Macha, shuddering in fear,
Had scented death, and pranced with fearsome noise,
But when it heard Cuchullin's chiding voice,
Meekly it sought the chariot to be bound,
And wept big tears of blood before him on the ground

Elves and Heroes

Then to his chariot leapt the lord of war
'O leave me not!' Levarchan cried in woe,
Thrice fifty queens, who gather'd from afar,
Moan'd with one voice, 'Ah, would'st thou from us go?'
They smote their hands, and fast their tears did flow—
Cuchullin's chariot thunder'd o'er the plain
Full well he knew that he would ne'er return again

How vehement and how beautiful they swept—
The Grey of Macha and the Black most bold
And keen-eyed Laegh, the watchful and adept,
Nor turn'd, nor spake, as on the chariot roll'd
The steeds he urged with his red goad of gold
Stooping he drave, with wing'd cloak and spheres,
Slender and tall and red—the King of Charioteers!

Cuchullin stood impatient for the fray,
His golden hilted bronze sword on his thigh
A sharp and venomous dart beside him lay,
He clasp'd his ashen spear, bronze-tipp'd and high,
As flames the sun upon the western sky,
His round shield from afar was flashing bright,
Figured with radiant gold and rimm'd with silver white

Stern-lipp'd he stood, his great broad head thrown back,
The white pearls sprayed upon his thick, dark hair,
Deep set, his eyes, beneath his eyebrows black,
Were swift and grey, and fix'd his fearless stare,
Red-edg'd his white hood flamed, his tunic rare
Of purple gleam'd with gold, his cloak behind
His shoulders shone with silver, floating in the wind

Betimes three crones him meet upon the way,
Half-blind and evil-eyed, with matted hair—
Workers of spells and witcheries are they—
The brood of Calatin—beware! beware!
They proffer of their fulsome food a share,
And, 'Stay with us a while,' a false crone cries
'Unseemly is the strong who would the weak despise'

He fain would pass, but leapt upon the ground,
The proud, the fearless! for sweet honour's sake—
With spells and poisons had they cook'd a hound,

Elves and Heroes

Of which he was forbidden to partake
But his name-charm the brave Cuchullin brake,
And their foul food he in his left hand took —
Eftsoons his former strength that arm and side forsook

For, O Cuchullin! could'st thou ere forget,
When fast by Culann's fort on yon black night,
Thou fought'st and slew the ban-dog dark as jet,
Which scared the thief, and put the foe to flight!
A tender youth thou wert of warrior might,
And all the land did with thy fame resound,
As Cathbad, the magician, named thee 'Culann's hound'

Loud o'er Mid Luachair road the chariot roll'd,
Round Shab Fuad desolate and grand,
Till Ere with hate the hero did behold,
Hast'ning to sweep the foemen from the land,
His sword flash'd red and radiant in his hand,
In sunny splendour was his spear upraised,
And hovering o'er his head the light of heroes blazed

He comes! he comes!' cried Ere as he drew near
'Await him, Men of Erin, and be strong!'
Their faces blanch'd, their bodies shook with fear —
'Now link thy shields and close together throng,
And shout the war-cry loud and fierce and long
Then Ere, with cunning of his evil heart,
Set heroes forth in pairs to feign to fight apart

As furious tempests, that in deep woods roar
Assault the giant trees and lay them low,
As billows toss the seaweed on the shore,
As sweeping sickles do the ripe fields mow —
Cuchullin, rolling fiercely on the foe,
Broke through the linked ranks upon the plain,
To drench the field with blood and round him heap the slain

And when he reach'd a warrior-pair that stood
In feignèd strife upon a knoll of green,
Their weapons clashing but unstained with blood,
A satirist him besought to intervene,
Whereat he slew them as he drave between —
"Thy spear to me," the satirist cried the while,

Elves and Heroes

The hero answering, "Nay," he cried, "I'll thee revile."

'Reviled for churlishness I ne'er have been,"
Cuchullin call'd, up-rising in his pride,
And cast his ashen spear bronze-tipp'd and keen
And slew the satirist and nine beside,
Then his fresh onslaught made the host divide
And flee before him clamouring with fear,
The while the stealthy Lugaid seized Cuchullin's spear

"O sons of Calatin," did Lugaid call,
"What falleth by the weapon I hold here?"
Together they acclaim'd, "A King will fall,
For so foretold," they said, "the aged seer."
Then at the chariot he flung the spear,
And Laegh was stricken unto death and fell
Cuchullin drew the spear and bade a last farewell

"The victor I, and eke the charioteer!"
He cried, and drave the war-steeds fierce and fast.
Another pair he slew, "To me thy spear,"
Again a satirist call'd. The spear was cast,
And through the satirist and nine men pass'd
But Lugaid grasps it, and again doth call,—
"What falleth by this spear?" They shout, "A King will fall"

"Then fall," cried Lugaid, as he flung the spear—
The Grey of Macha sank in death's fierce throes,
Snapping the yoke, the while the Black ran clear:
Cuchullin groan'd, and dash'd upon his foes;
Another pair he slew with rapid blows,
And eke the satirist and nine men near:
Then once more Lugaid sprang to seize the charmèd spear.

"What falleth by this weapon?" he doth call
"A King will fall," they answer him again ...
"But twice before ye said, 'A King will fall'" ...
They cried, "The King of Steeds hath fled the plain,
And lo, the King of Charioteers is slain!" ...
For the last time he drave the spear full well,
And smote the great Cuchullin—and Cuchullin fell

The Black steed snapp'd the yoke, and left alone

Elves and Heroes

The King of Heroes dying on the plain:
"I fain would drink," they heard Cuchullin groan,
"From out yon loch" ... He thirsted in fierce pain.
"We give thee leave, but thou must come again,"
His foemen said; then low made answer he,
"If I will not return, I'll bid you come to me"

His wound he bound, and to the loch did hie,
And drank his drink, and wash'd, and made no moan.
Then came the brave Cuchullin forth to die,
Sublimely fearless, strengthless and alone ...
He wended to the standing pillar-stone,
Clutching his sword and leaning on his spear,
And to his foemen called, "Come ye, and meet me here."

A vision swept upon his fading brain—
A passing vision glorious and sweet,
That hour of youth return'd to him again
When he took arms with fearless heart a-beat,
As Cathbad, the magician, did repeat,
"Who taketh arms upon this day of grief,
His name shall live forever and his life be brief"

Fronting his foes, he stood with fearless eye,
His body to the pillar-stone he bound,
Nor sitting nor down-lying would he die ...
He would die standing ... so they gathered round
In silent wonder on the blood-drench'd ground,
And watch'd the hero who with Death could strive;
But no man durst approach ... He seem'd to be alive ...

LOST SONGS.

Harp of my fathers—on the mouldering wall
  Of days forgotten—like a far-off wind
Hushing the fir-wood at soft even-fall,
  Thy low-heard whispers to my heart recall
The wistful songs, to Silence Old consigned,
  That Ossian sang when he was frail and blind.

Thy fitful notes from the melodious trees,
  I fain would echo in my feeble rhyme—
The inner music quivering on the breeze
  I hear; and throbbing from the beating seas,
On ancient shores, the wearied pulse of Time
  That mingles with thy melodies sublime.

OTHER POEMS.

THE DREAM.

'Twas when I woke I knew it was a dream,
Measured by moments, that to me did seem,
  A life-long spell of joy and peace to be—

Will that last dream that comes ere death descends,
From which I shall not wake to know it ends,
  Thus seem to live on through Eternity?

FREE WILL.

Say not the will of man is free
  Within the limits of his soul—
Who from his heritage can flee?
  Who can his destiny control?

In vain we wage perpetual strife,
  'Gainst instincts dumb and blind desires—
Who leads must serve.. The pulse of life
  Throbs with the dictates of our sires.

Since when the world began to be,
  And life through hidden purpose came,
From sire to son unceasingly
  The task bequeathed hath been the same.

We strive, while fetters bind us fast,
  We seek to do what needs must be—
We move through bondage with the past
  In service to posterity.

STRIFE.

Weary of strife—
The surge and clash of city life—
I sought for peace in solitude,
Within the hushed and darkened wood
And on the lonesome moor—
But found contending leaf and root
Engaged in conflict fierce though mute,
While what was frail was slain
By what was strong in dire dispute—
I sought for peace in vain!
The world, sustained by strife, endures in pain.

"All things that are in conflict be,"
I murmured on the shelving strand,
Where struggling winds would fain be free—
The tides in conflict with the wind's command,
Turned tossing, wearily—
I heard the loud sea labouring to the land—
I saw the dumb land striving with the sea.

SONNET.

(Written in the Stone Gallery of St Paul's.)

The drowsing city sparkles in the heat,
And murmur in mine ears unceasingly
The surging tides of that vast human sea—
The billows of life that break with muffled beat
And vibrate through this high and lone retreat;
While over all, serene, and fair, and free,
Thy dome is reared in naked majesty
Grey, old St Paul's ... In thee the Ages meet,
Slumbering amidst the trophies of their strife.
And in their dreams thou hearest, while the cries
Of triumph and despair ascend from Life,
The murmurings of immortality—
Thou Sentinel of Hope that doth despise
What was and is not, waiting what shall be!

"OUT OF THE MOUTHS OF BABES."

"Is baby dead?" he whispered, with wide eyes
  Tearless, but full of eloquent regret,
His childish face grown prematurely wise —
  Pond'ring the problem death before him set.

"Baby is dead," I answered, as I laid
  My hand on her frail forehead with a sigh;
"Oh! daddy, why did God do this?" he said,
  And silently my heart made answer, "Why?"

He touched her white, worn face, and said, "How cold
  Is our wee baby now." ... His eyes were deep ...
Then came his little brother, two years old,
  He looked, and lisped, "The baby is asleep."

NOTES.

The Wee Folk. —In Gaelic they are usually called "The Peace People" (sithchean). Other names are "Wee Folk" (daoine beaga); "Light Folk" (slaugh eutrom), etc. As in the Lowlands, they are also referred to as "guid fowk" and "guid neighbours."

The Banshee (Beanshith). —Sometimes referred to as "The Fairy Queen," sometimes as "The Green Lady." She sings a song while she washes the clothes of one about to meet a swift and tragic fate. In the Fian poems she converses with those who see her, and foretells the fate of warriors going to battle.

The Blue Men of the Minch (Na Fir Ghorm). —Between the Shant Isles (Charmed Isles) and Lewis is the "Stream of the Blue Men." They are the "sea-horses" of the island Gaels. Their presence in the strait was believed to be the cause of its billowy restlessness and swift currents.

The Changeling. —When the fairies robbed a mother of her babe, they left behind a useless, old, and peevish fairy, who took the form of a child. This belief may have originated in the assumption that when a baby became ill and fretful, it was a changeling.

The Urisk is, if anything, a personification of fear. It is a silent, cloudy shape which haunts lonely moors, and follows travellers, but rarely does more than scare them.

My Fairy Lover. —Fairies fell in love with human beings, and deserted them when their love was returned. Women of unsound mind, given to wandering alone in solitary places, were believed to be the victims of fairy love.

Yon Fairy Dog (An Cu Sith) was heard howling on stormy nights. He was "big as a stirk," one informant has declared The "fearsome tail" appears to have been not the least impressive thing about it. The MacCodrums were brave and fearless, and were supposed to be descended from Seals, which were believed to be human beings under spells.

My Gunna. —This kindly, but solitary, elf herded cattle by night, and prevented them from falling over the rocks. He was seen only by those gifted with the faculty of "second sight." The Gunna resembles the Lowland "Brownie."

Her Evil Eye. —Belief in the Evil Eye is still quite common, even among educated people, in the Highlands. Not a few children wear "the cord," to which a silver coin is appended, as a charm against the influence of "the eye."

The Little Old Man of the Barn (Bodachan Sabhaill). —Like the Gunna, he is a variety the kindly Brownie, and assisted the needy.

Nimble Men (Na Fir Chlis) are "The Merry Dancers," or Aurora Borealis. It was believed that, when the streamers were coloured, the "men and maids" were dancing, and that after the dance the lovers fought for the love of the queen. When the streamers are particularly vivid, a pink cloud is seen below them, and this is called "the pool of blood." It drips upon blood-stones, the spots on which are referred to as fairy blood (fuil siochaire). A wizard could, by waving his wand, summon the "Nimble Men" to dance in the northern sky.

The Water Horse haunted lonely lochs, and lured human beings to a terrible death. When a hand was laid on its main, power to remove it was withdrawn.

A Cursing—The Gaelic curses are quaint in translation, but terrible in the original.

Bonnach Fallaidh. —It was considered unlucky to throw away the remnants of a baking. So the good-wife made a little bannock, which was pierced in the middle, as a charm against fairy influence. It was given to a child for performing an errand, but the charm would be broken if the reason for gifting it were explained. That was the good-wife's secret. It was also unlucky to count the bannocks, and when they fell, "bad luck" was foretold. Finlay's bannock was not kneaded on the board or placed on the brander, but, unlike the other bannocks, was toasted in front of the fire.

The Gruagach was a gentlemanly Brownie, who haunted byres. It was never seen, although its shadow occasionally danced on the wall as it flitted about. Often, when chased, it was heard tittering round corners. In some barns, Clach-na-gruagach—"the Gruagach's stone"—is still seen. Milkers pour an offering of milk into the hollowed stone "for luck." The cream might not rise and the churn yield no butter if this service were neglected. A favourite trick of the Gruagach was to untie the cattle in the byre, so as to bring out the milkmaid, especially if she had forgotten to leave the offering of milk.

Tober Mhuire (St Mary's Well) is situated at Tarradale, Ross-shire. When a sick person asks for a drink of Tober Mhuire water, it is taken as a sign of approaching death. It is a curious thing that this reverence for holy water should be perpetuated among a Presbyterian people. Wishing and curative wells are numerous in the North.

The Fians of Knockfarrel. —This story belongs to the Ossianic or Fian cycle of Gaelic tales in prose and verse. Hugh Miller makes reference to it, but speaks of the Fians as giants. In Strathpeffer district the tale is well known, and it is referred to in "Waifs and Strays of Celtic Tradition. " It is also localised in Skye. There are several Fian place-names in the Highlands. The warriors are supposed to lie in a charmed sleep in Craig-a-howe Cave, near Munlochy, Ross-shire. Caoilte, the swift runner, was a famous Fian. Finn was chief, and Goll and Garry were of Clan Morna, which united with the Fians. "Moolachie" is a little babe, and "clarsach, " a harp.

Ledbag's Warning. —Children who twist their mouths, or squint, are warned that, if the wind changes, their contortions will remain. The fate of the flounder, which mocked the cod, is cited as a terrible example.

Conn, Son of the Red is a Fian tale of which several old Gaelic versions have been collected. Goll, the "first hero" of the Fians, slew the Red when Conn, his son, was seven years old. In the fullness of time the young hero, whom his enemies admire as well as fear, crossed the sea to avenge his father's death, and engaged in a long and fierce duel with Goll.

Death of Cuchullin is from the Cuchullin Cycle of Bronze Age heroic tales. The enemy have invaded and laid waste the province of Ulster, and the chief warriors of the Red Branch, except Cuchullin, who must needs fight alone, are laid under spells by the magicians of the invaders. The poem is suffused with evidences of magical beliefs and practices. Cuchullin goes forth knowing that he will meet his doom. His name signifies "hound of Culann. " In his youth he slew Culann's ferocious watch-hound which attacked him, and took its place until another was trained. It was "geis" (taboo) for him to partake of the flesh of a hound (his totem), or eat at a cooking hearth; but he must needs accept the hospitality of the witches. The satirists are satirical bards who, it was believed, could not only lampoon a hero, but infuse their compositions with magical powers like incantations. Cuchullin cannot be slain except by his own spear, which he must deliver up to a satirist who demands it. Emania, the capital of Ulster, was the home of the Bed Branch warriors.

Sleepy Song. —When Diarmid eloped with Grianne, as Paris did with Helen, the Fians followed them, so that Finn, their chief, might be avenged. Diarmid, who is the unwilling victim of Grainne's spells, dreads to meet Finn, and is in constant fear of discovery.